Journey of the Nightly Jaguar

INSPIRED BY
AN ANCIENT MAYAN MYTH

by

BURTON ALBERT

illustrated
by

ROBERT ROTH

atheneum books for young readers

TO SHERRY
whose sunshine warms many a path
and
TO HEATHER AND MICHAEL
whose journey is just beginning
—B. A.

For my wife, Cheryl, and daughter, Cassidy,
with love
—R. R.

Atheneum Books for Young Readers
An imprint of Simon & Schuster Children's Publishing Division
1230 Avenue of the Americas
New York, New York 10020

Designed by Angela Carlino

First edition

Printed in the United States of America

10 9 8 7 6 5 4 3 2 1

The text of this book is set in 18 point Beatsville

The illustrations are rendered in watercolor

Albert, Burton.
Journey of the nightly jaguar : inspired by an ancient Mayan myth
by Burton Albert ; illustrated by Robert Roth.—1st ed.
p.   cm.
Summary: In this Mayan legend the sun becomes a jaguar at night,
stalking through the jungle until it appears again as the sun in the
eastern sky.
ISBN 0-689-31905-3
1. Mayas—Folklore. 2. Tales—Central America. 3. Jaguar—Folklore. [1. Mayas—Folklore.
2. Indians of Central America—Folklore.] I. Roth, Robert, ill. II. Title.
F.1435.3.F6A43 1995
398.2'097281'0452974428—dc20   94-14456

Thousands and thousands of moons ago,
Maya Indians were already living in Central America.
To them, happenings in nature—
the wind and the rain
and the sprouting of crops—
were caused by gods.

The gods sometimes took on the forms of animals.
One was the jaguar.
A creature with a loud, deep roar
and silent ways of attack,
it was among the most feared
—and therefore godlike—
in the Mayan world.

This tale links
the strong and beautiful beast
to the mystery of the sun.

Again, at the edge of the Mayan forest,

raindrops—like golden coins—

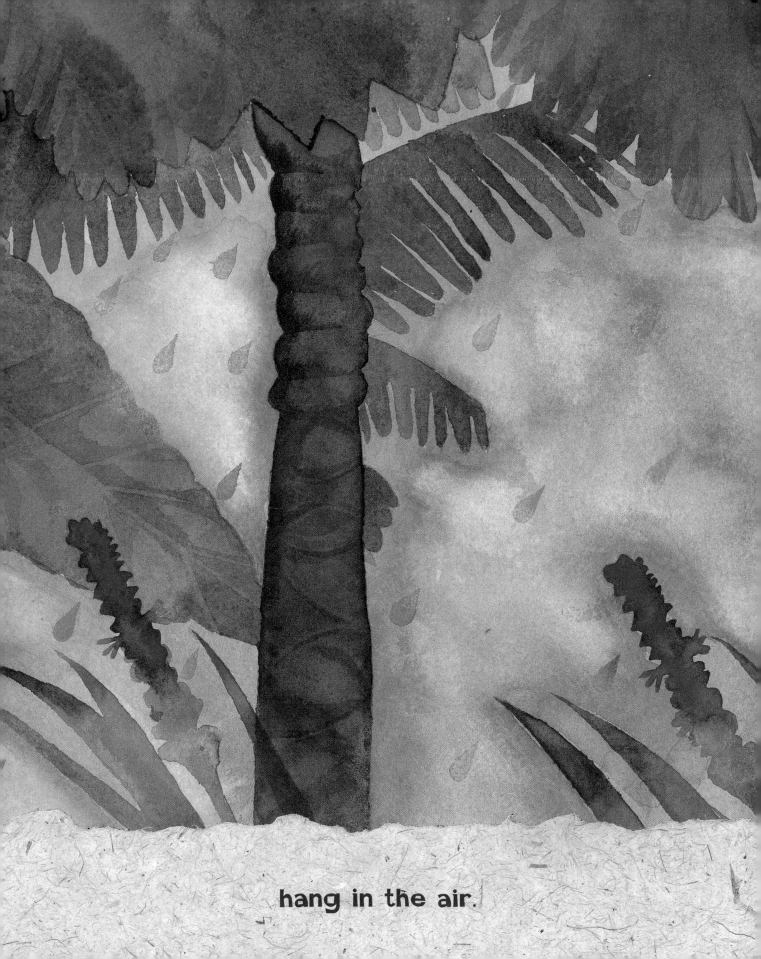

hang in the air.

And again, as the sun sets,

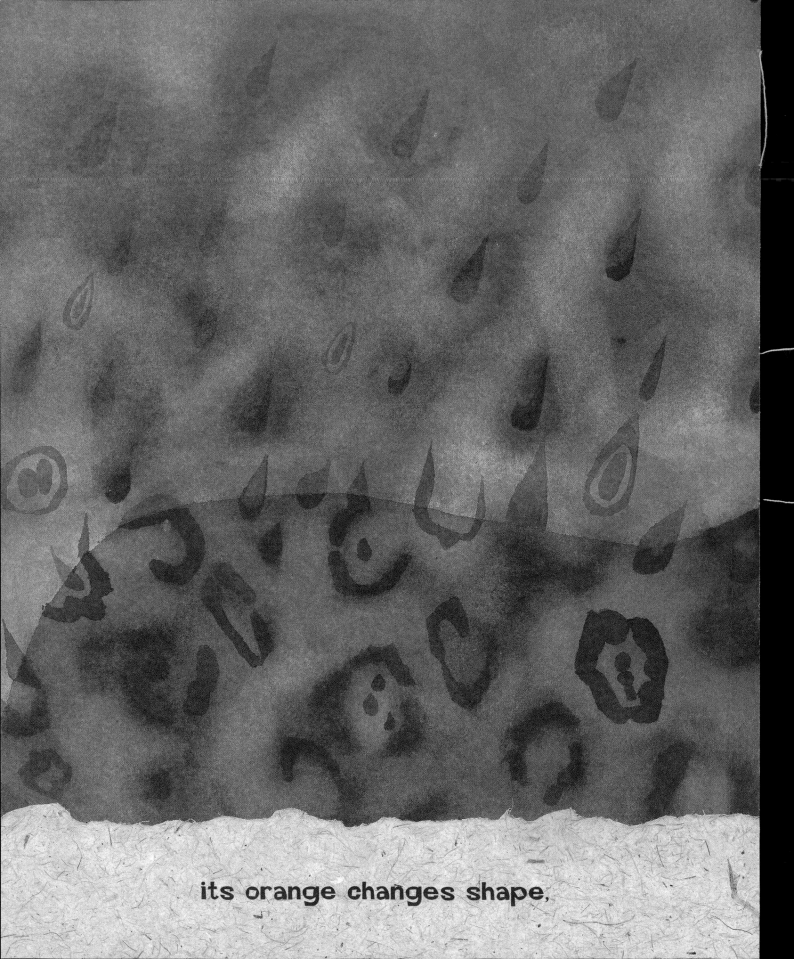

its orange changes shape,

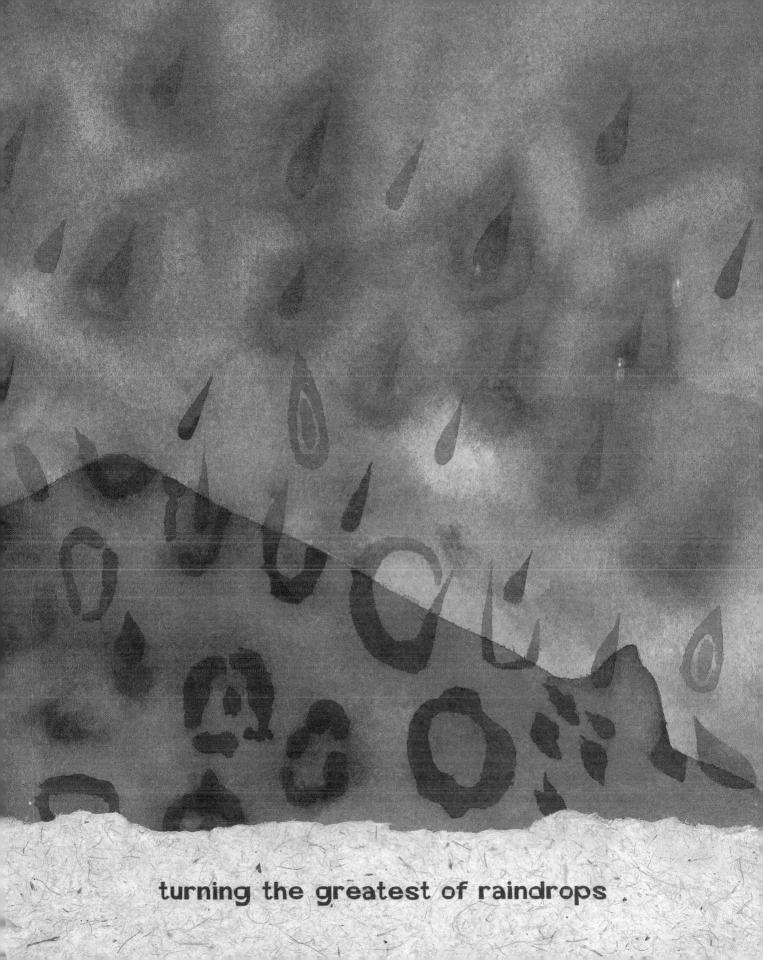

turning the greatest of raindrops

into the ebony markings of a nightly jaguar.

And again, windsongs from the east.

whistle through the trees,

luring the creature on his journey of return

through cascades of leafy umbrellas,

jungles of knotted vines,

and the chatterings of a million monkeys.

And again, the creature stalks the
moonlit mountains,

the star-studded valleys,

and the winding rivers of crocodile eyes.

And again, near journey's end, he bounds
up a towering trunk,

where he hides in a cloudy canopy

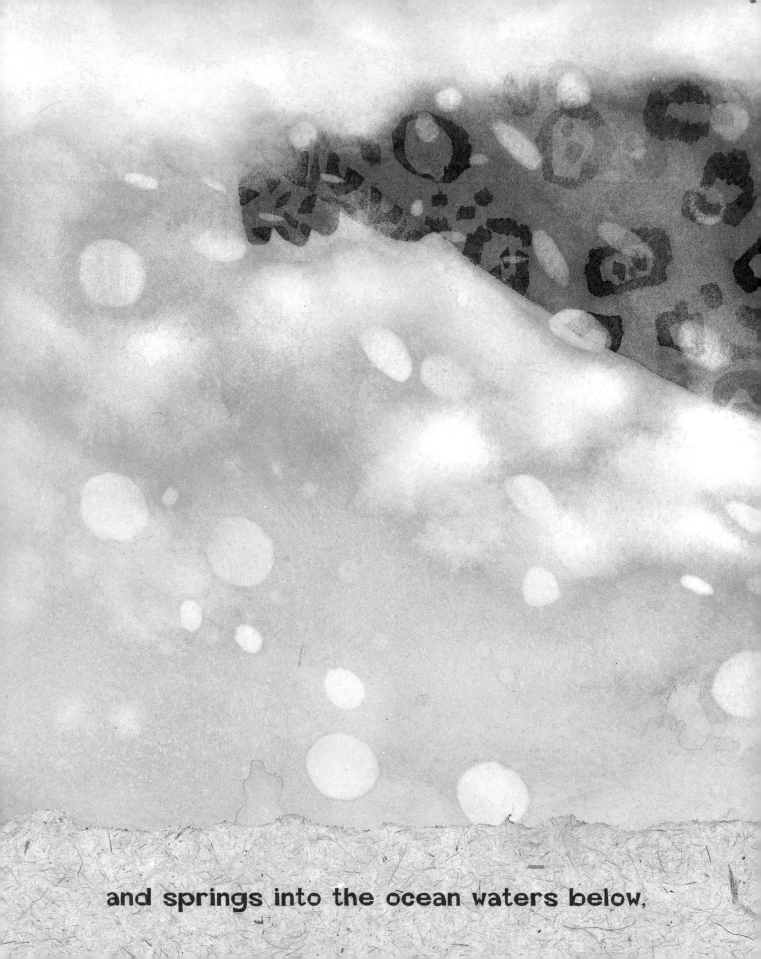

and springs into the ocean waters below,

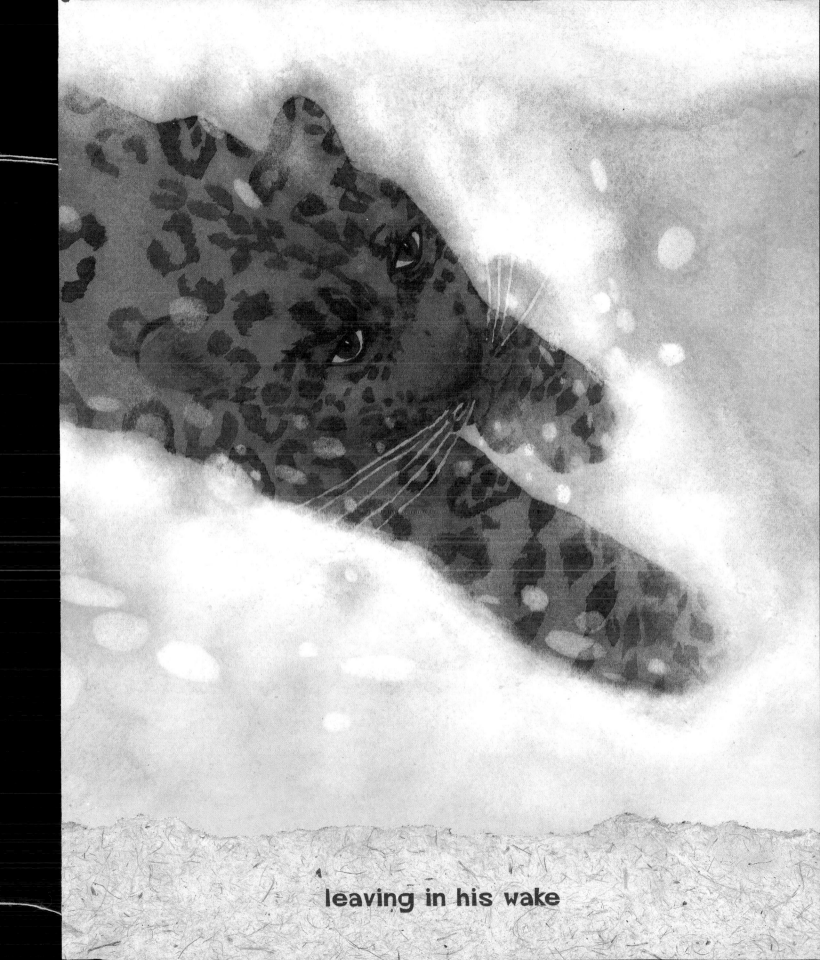

leaving in his wake

a spray of shimmering bubbles

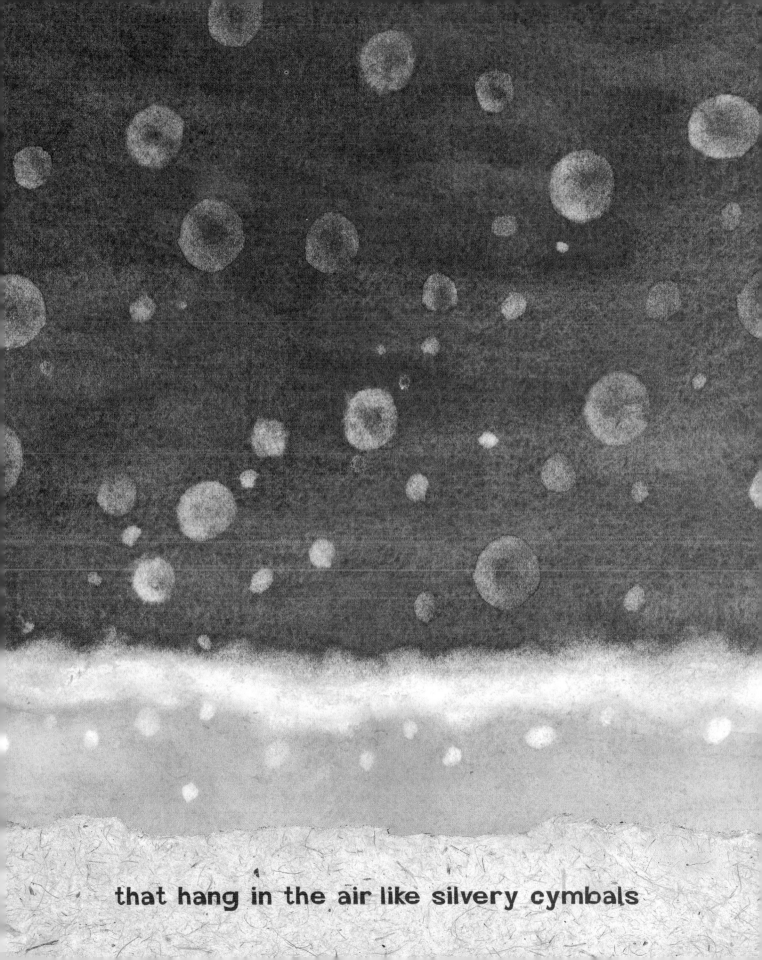

that hang in the air like silvery cymbals

till that one magical moment

when this cat of the night

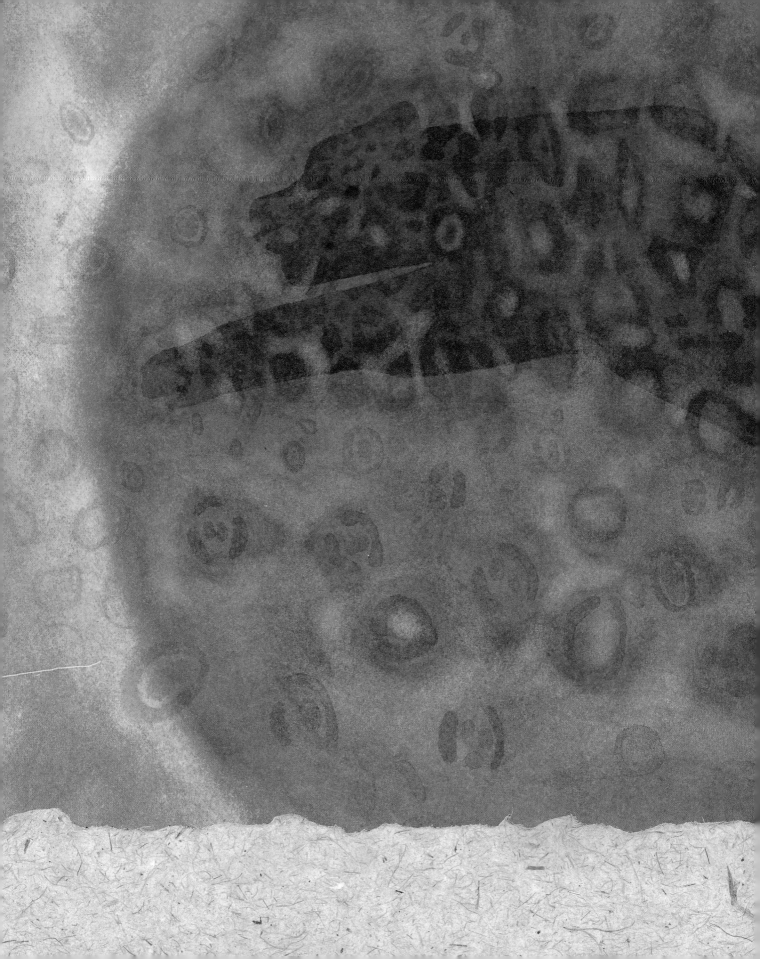

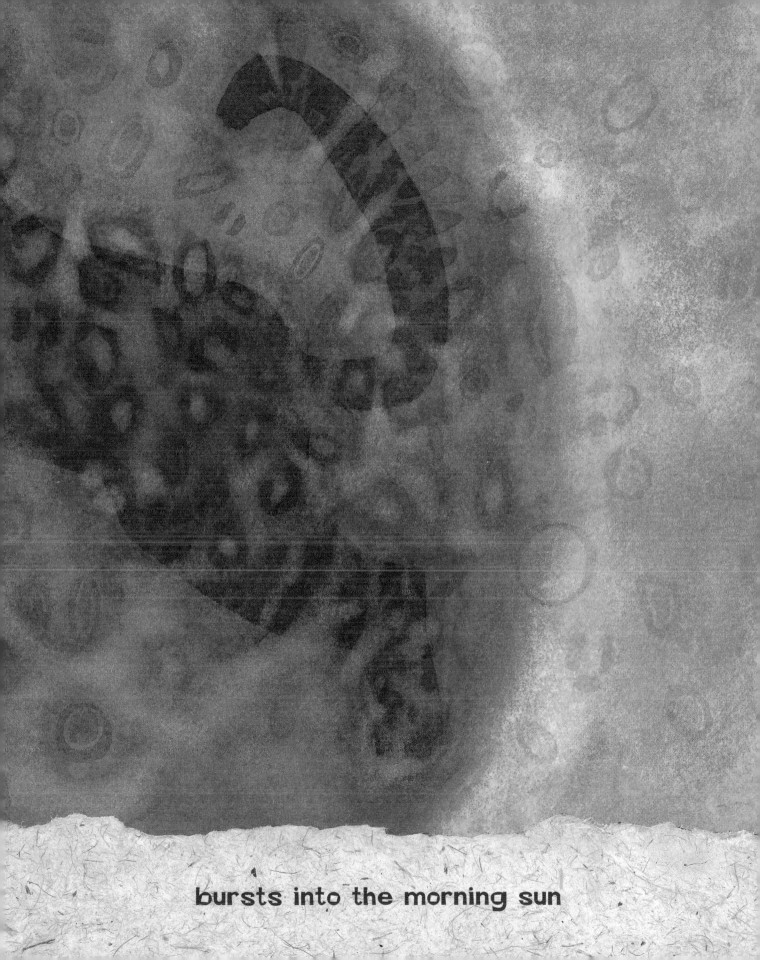

bursts into the morning sun

and rises a glorious red ... once again.

Today the life of the jaguar hangs in the balance.
It is an endangered species.

Ranchers kill it to keep it from cattle.
Villagers kill it to defend themselves.
Others kill it for a head on the wall,
a rug to walk on, a fur to wear.
Some even capture the young for pets.

But in Belize, a country of Central America,
a refuge signals hope.
It is called the Cockscomb Jaguar Preserve.
There, the great creature of the legend—
protected from the attack of humans—
slowly but steadily multiplies.